Magic Growing Powder

by JANET QUIN-HARKIN

pictures by ART CUMINGS

PARENTS MAGAZINE PRESS • NEW YORK

Text Copyright © 1980 by Janet Quin-Harkin.
Illustrations Copyright © 1980 by Art Cumings.
All rights reserved.
Printed in the United States of America.
10 9 8 7 6 5 4 3 2 1

Library of Congress Cataloging in Publication Data
Quin-Harkin, Janet.   Magic growing powder.
SUMMARY: Despondent over being short, King Max
promises half his kingdom and his daughter's hand
for some magic growing powder.
[1. Fairy tales.   2. Size and shape—Fiction]
I. Cumings, Art.   II. Title.   PZ8.Q55 Mag [E] 80–18019
ISBN 0–8193–1037–9   ISBN 0–8193–1038–7   (lib. bdg.)

for Leona Devine, with thanks

Once there was a king named Max.
He was very, very short.
King Max hated being short,
although no one else seemed to mind.

He spent all his time trying
to make himself taller.

He hung by his hands
from the lights.
But that just hurt his arms.
He hung by his feet, too.

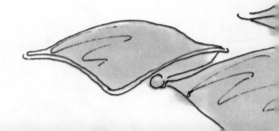

He ate bowl after bowl of spinach,
until he began to turn green.
But nothing made him taller.
So King Max sat and sulked all day.

He sent his whole court away,
and filled the palace
with strange people
who promised to make him taller.

His only child, Princess Penny,
was very sad.
"Father," she said,
"there is no one to rule your kingdom."

But the king would not listen to her.
So things got worse and worse.

One day two strangers came
to see the king.
"Your Majesty," they said,
"we have brought you this."
And they opened a small wooden box.

"What is it?" asked King Max.
"It looks like a box of sand."

"Magic Growing Powder,"
  said the strangers.
"When some of this falls onto
  a living thing, it grows overnight."

"How much does the powder cost?"
  asked the king.
"Half of your kingdom,"
  said one of the strangers.
"And your daughter's hand in marriage,"
  said the other.
"Cheap at the price," said the king.

Princess Penny did not
believe the strangers.
And she did not
want to marry either one.
"Now, wait a minute, Father,"
she said.
"We must test the powder first."

"Very well," said the king.

The strangers went to the window
and sprinkled some powder onto
the daisies below.
"Just wait overnight,"
said the strangers.

At night they dug up the daisies
and planted sunflowers.

Sure enough, by morning,
there were flowers reaching
to the window ledge.

"I'll take the powder," said the king.
"Just a minute!" said the princess.
"It worked on flowers.
But does it work on anything else?
We must try it again."

"Oh, very well," said the king.
So the strangers sprinkled some on the palace cat.
They shut it in the cellar for the night.

While everyone else was asleep,
they brought in a tiger instead.

Next morning, a deep growl came from the cellar.
"Goodness!" shouted the king. "That cat is huge!
The powder works!
Bring me half my kingdom!"

"Just a minute, Father,"
said Princess Penny.
"You wouldn't want to
grow too tall, would you?
Look how large those flowers
and that cat grew.
Try the powder on these men first.
Then we shall know
the correct dose for a person."
"Good idea," said the king.

But the strangers didn't think so.
They looked unhappy when the king
sprinkled powder on their heads.
They looked unhappy when guards
locked them in their room for the night.
But in a few minutes they fell asleep.

"So far, so good," said Princess Penny.
She had put a sleeping powder into their wine.
When all was quiet, she crept out of the palace
and called together all the carpenters
and all the tailors
and all the shoemakers.

They made two tiny beds.

They made tiny shoes . . .

and tiny clothes.

They lowered the ceiling.

In the morning
when the two strangers woke up,
they were hanging over
the ends of their beds.
They leaped up
and banged their heads
on the ceiling.
They tried to get dressed,
but their clothes
were much too tiny.

"Help! Help! We've turned into giants!"
screamed the two men.
They leaped out the window,
ran away, and were never seen again.

Princess Penny told her father
what she had done.
"What a fool I have been," he sighed.
"I should quit right now
 and let you be queen."

"Rubbish," said Princess Penny.
"Being short doesn't matter.
 You can be a good king if you try."

So King Max called back all the court.
He worked so hard at being a good king
that he didn't have time to notice he was short.
And what's more, his people didn't notice
he was short either.

JANET QUIN-HARKIN has had a very busy life, living in several countries and working at many interesting jobs. Born in England, she studied there and in Austria and Germany. She wrote and performed in shows, played guitar and sang in a folk club, worked for the BBC in London and the Australian Broadcasting Company in Sydney—and even managed a rock group.

Mrs. Quin-Harkin and her husband now live in California with their four children. She has been writing newspaper and magazine articles and children's books. She says, "My close connection with the theater and radio has shaped my writing. My picture books are made up of comic scenes that could easily be turned into a play."

Magic Growing Powder is Janet Quin-Harkin's third book for Parents, following *Benjamin's Balloon* and *Septimus Bean and His Amazing Machine*.

ART CUMINGS's background in animated cartoons helped him develop his keen sense of how to move a story along visually. His lively book illustrations seem ready to jump off the page into action in a cartoon feature— just right for Janet Quin-Harkin's theatrical stories. In fact, he illustrated her *Septimus Bean and His Amazing Machine* in addition to two other Parents books.

Mr. Cumings has also done magazine and advertising illustration and is now turning to writing children's books as well. He and his family live in Douglaston, New York.